Will Jax Be Home for Thanksgiving?

Written by Samarrah Fine Clayman
Illustrated by Amy Preveza

Dear Reader,

This book comes from my heart. In 2017, my 23-month-old son was diagnosed with a rare brain tumor found mainly in young children.

While my son was in the hospital recovering, I searched everywhere for children's books to share with him and his five-year old sister. I never found one that spoke to me or my family. As a writer, a social worker and a mother, I decided to meet that need for other families faced with illness.

This story is about gratitude and a celebration of life––no matter what. No one can predict what life has in store for us. So we must always celebrate the gift of a new day.

Warmly,
Samarrah

All profits from the sale of this book will be donated to The Ependymoma Research Foundation. After her son's diagnosis, Samarrah and her husband created this nonprofit foundation to support research for pediatric brain tumors, with the goal of a cure.
You can learn more at: www.BrainTumorWarrior.org

For Dr. Edward Robert Smith,
Dr. Karen Wright, and Dr. Torunn Yock

Printed in the United States of America

First Printing, 2019

Ependymoma Research Foundation
1337 Massachusetts Ave. #219
Arlington, MA 02476

ISBN-13: 978-0-578-55473-0
LCCN: 2019911134

Book Design: Tobi Carter

My brother, Jax, is three.
I'm Lyla, and I'm seven.
Jax has blonde hair.
Mine is brown.
He's in the hospital.
I'm not.

In early November,
Jax needed surgery.
"He has a marble-sized lump
growing inside his head,"
Mom explained.
"It's called a brain tumor."

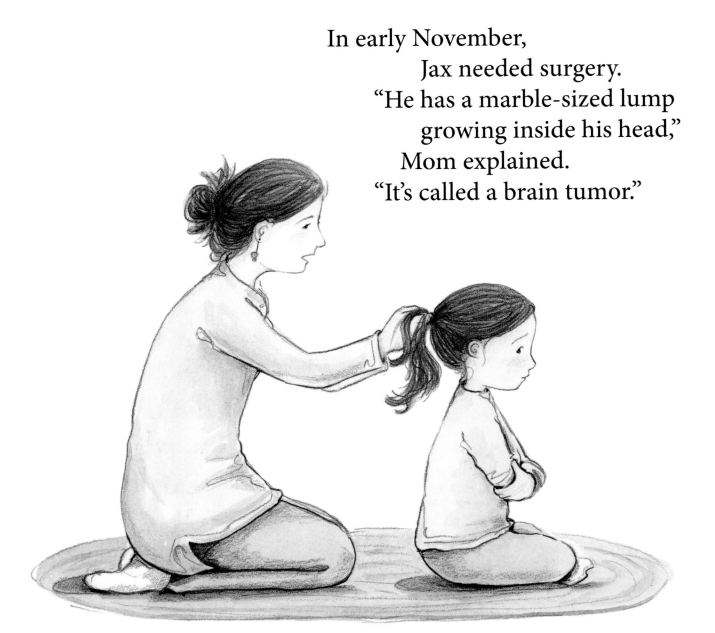

I don't have a tumor. No one else in our family does.
Why does Jax have one?
"Some people just get them," said Mom.

Before the surgery, the doctors gave Jax medicine to make him sleep.
Dad said Jax didn't feel anything when they took out the tumor.
When he woke up, the marble-sized lump was gone.

Now, Jax has to stay in the hospital
until the doctors say he can come home.
I miss him.

I hope he comes home
before Thanksgiving.
It's our favorite holiday.
Jax and I make
decorations together
and help Mom
make apple pie.

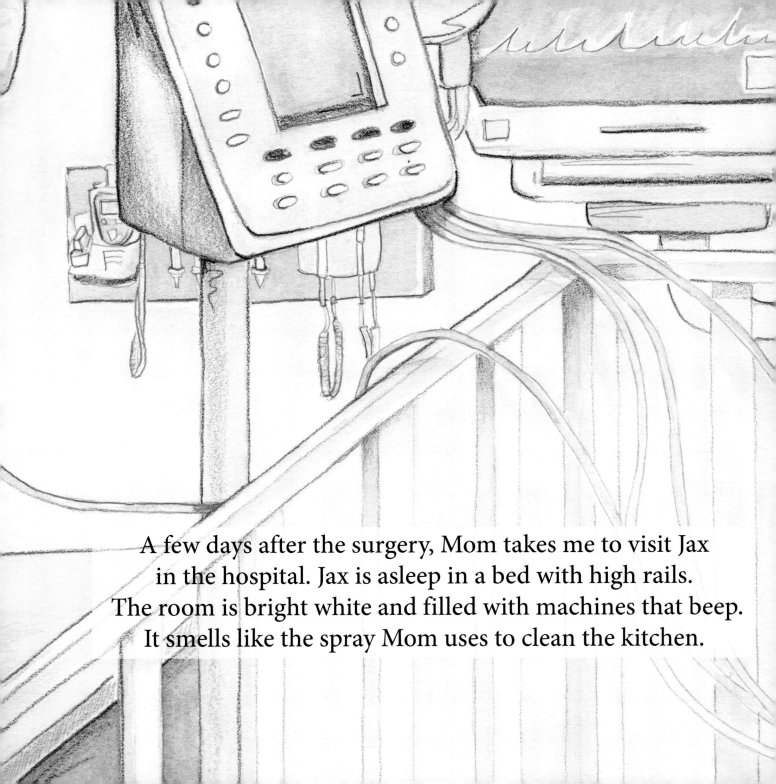

A few days after the surgery, Mom takes me to visit Jax
in the hospital. Jax is asleep in a bed with high rails.
The room is bright white and filled with machines that beep.
It smells like the spray Mom uses to clean the kitchen.

"Hi Jax!" I try to smile. "I brought you a new stuffy."
He hugs it. Then he closes his eyes.

Where is my loud, silly brother? I want him to wake up!

I have so many questions. Are the doctors nice?
How is the food? Do you get to bring the books and toys home?
Will you be home for Thanksgiving?

Dad walks into the room.
He slept at the hospital last
night with Jax.
Mom and Dad take turns.
"I missed you, Dad" I say.
"I missed you too, Lyla.
I'll be home tonight."
I'm glad Dad
is coming home.
But I want all of us
to be home together.

On the way home, I ask Dad, "Is Jax OK?
He looks different, and he's so sleepy."
"I know it's scary to see Jax in the hospital," he says.
"But he'll get better. It just takes time."

The next week, Mom and Dad still take turns sleeping at the hospital. Sometimes after school, I visit Jax, too.

A week before Thanksgiving, Jax is ready to come home.
When we pick him up, he looks pale but happy.

As soon as we get home, Jax falls asleep on the couch.
Mom makes his favorite dinner--macaroni and cheese.
I gobble mine up, but Jax doesn't eat anything,
not even dessert.

The next day, Dad rakes the yard.
I wish Jax could jump in a leaf pile
with me. But he still needs
to stay inside and rest.
I say, "Jax, come help me collect leaves
for Thanksgiving decorations."
"I'm too tired, Lyla," Jax says yawning.
Will Jax be able to enjoy Thanksgiving?

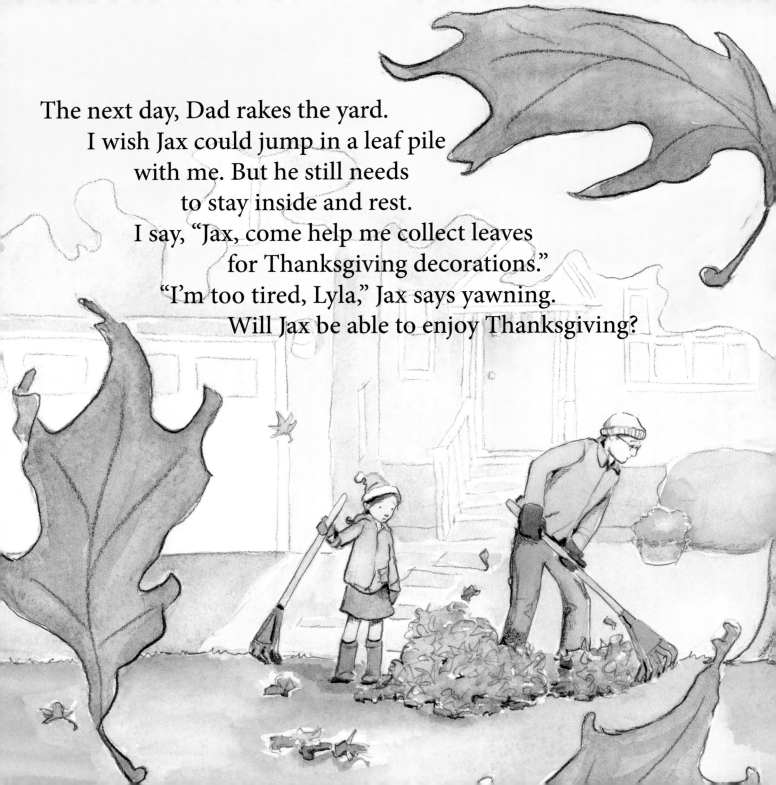

In the living room, I build a fort for us with couch cushions.
Jax crawls in, then falls asleep snuggled next to me.

"When will Jax run around and play with me?" I ask mom.
"In a few weeks," she says. "Jax had a big surgery.
It takes time to recover."

Over the next few days,
Jax starts to feel better.
The day before
Thanksgiving,
I ask Mom,
"Can we make a pie?"
"Of course," says Mom.

"Apple!" says Jax.
"How much cinnamon should we add?" asks Mom.
"Double!" Jax and I say.

The house smells sweet.

Later, Jax and I trace our hands with crayons
to make paper turkeys.
We decorate the pictures
with feathers and glitter.
Jax smiles--the biggest smile since
he went to the hospital.
I smile back.
"Gobble, gobble," I say.
"Gobble, gobble," says Jax.

On Thanksgiving Day, we have turkey, mashed potatoes,
    and cranberry sauce. Mom lights candles.
    Jax picks up two corn muffins.
        He hands one to me and munches the other.
    I look around the table at my family.
I'm so thankful we're all together.

Samarrah Clayman a social worker and writer based in Lexington, Massachusetts, teaches yoga and meditation. According to her two children, she bakes the best chocolate chip cookies.

In 2017, Samarrah's 23-month-old son was diagnosed with an ependymoma—a brain tumor that can occur at any age, but most often in young children. The tumor can cause headaches, seizures and paralysis. The main treatment is surgery and radiation, though the tumors can often reoccur. There is no cure, but there is hope that with additional research, these tumors can be treated more successfully.

After her son's diagnosis, Samarrah and her husband created The Ependymoma Research Foundation. You can learn more at: www.BrainTumorWarrior.org

Find out more about Samarrah at www.SamarrahFineClayman.org

Amy Preveza is a children's book illustrator, a special education teacher, and an elementary and middle school art teacher. She works primarily in traditional media such as pencil, colored pencil, charcoal, watercolor, and occasionally oil pastel. She lives in Connecticut with her husband and three children. To see more of her work, visit www.amypreveza.com.